To the memory of
Grandma Sittenreich and Nana London, and for Peggy Dunn,
a teacher whose life is love.
— J.L.

To my grandmothers,
Sylvia Nichols Lyman and Margaret Mitchell Carlisle,
whose stars shine brightly still.
— S.L.

Book design by Laura Jane Coats. Typeset in Stempel Garamond and Charlemagne. Printed in Hong Kong.
Library of Congress Cataloging-in-Publication Data:
London, Jonathan, 1947–
Liplap's Wish / by Jonathan London; illustrated by Sylvia Long.
p. cm.
Summary: As he builds a snowbunny, Liplap feels something is missing
and wishes his grandmother, who recently died, was with him.
ISBN 0-8118-0505-0
[1. Rabbits — Fiction. 2. Grandmothers — Fiction. 3. Death — Fiction.] I. Long, Sylvia, ill. II. Title
PZ7.L8432Lj 1994 [E] — dc20 93-31007 CIP AC
Distributed in Canada by Raincoast Books, 8680 Cambie Street, Vancouver, British Columbia V6P 6M9
10 9 8 7 6 5 4 3
Chronicle Books
85 Second Street, San Francisco, California 94105
Website: www.chronbooks.com

LIPLAP'S WISH

written by

Jonathan London

illustrated by

Sylvia Long

chronicle books · san francisco

One winter morning, Liplap woke up and looked out his window. The first snowfall had covered his yard with a blanket of sparkling white!

He quickly tugged on his winter clothes and hopped outside — *lip-lap, lip-lap* — and got right down to work, rolling and shaping the snow. Soon he had made a snowbunny. But it didn't have a face.

"I wish," thought Liplap, "Grandma could see my snowbunny. She'd know how to make it look really great. She'd know how to give it a face."

But Grandma hadn't lived to see the snow this year. Liplap still couldn't believe it. He kept expecting to see her step from his house.

Liplap hopped back inside — *lip-lap, lip-lap* —
and rummaged in the old satin-lined box
where Grandma kept ribbons and bobbins
and knickknacks and things.

Then he hopped back outside
and poked in five different kinds of
buttons for the snowbunny's coat.
He still half hoped Grandma would
come out to see his snowbunny.

The front door opened.
His father waved and said, “Liplap!
Your snowbunny has no face!”

Suddenly, Liplap felt like crying.
He hopped right by his father
and back into bed.

Liplap's mother brought him carrot cake
and hot cocoa, still steaming,
but Liplap didn't feel like eating.
She patted his back, and sang him a lullaby
until he drifted off to sleep.

Later that day, Liplap once again looked out his window. The setting sun was pulling rose and yellow scarves across the sky. His snowbunny looked cold.

Liplap quickly bundled up again and hopped outside — *lip-lap, lip-lap*. He threw his own scarf around the snowbunny's shoulders, his rumpled cap on the snowbunny's head.

Liplap pulled off his mittens and slid them over the snowbunny's snow paws. He cupped his own cold little paws and blew on them the way Grandma used to do.

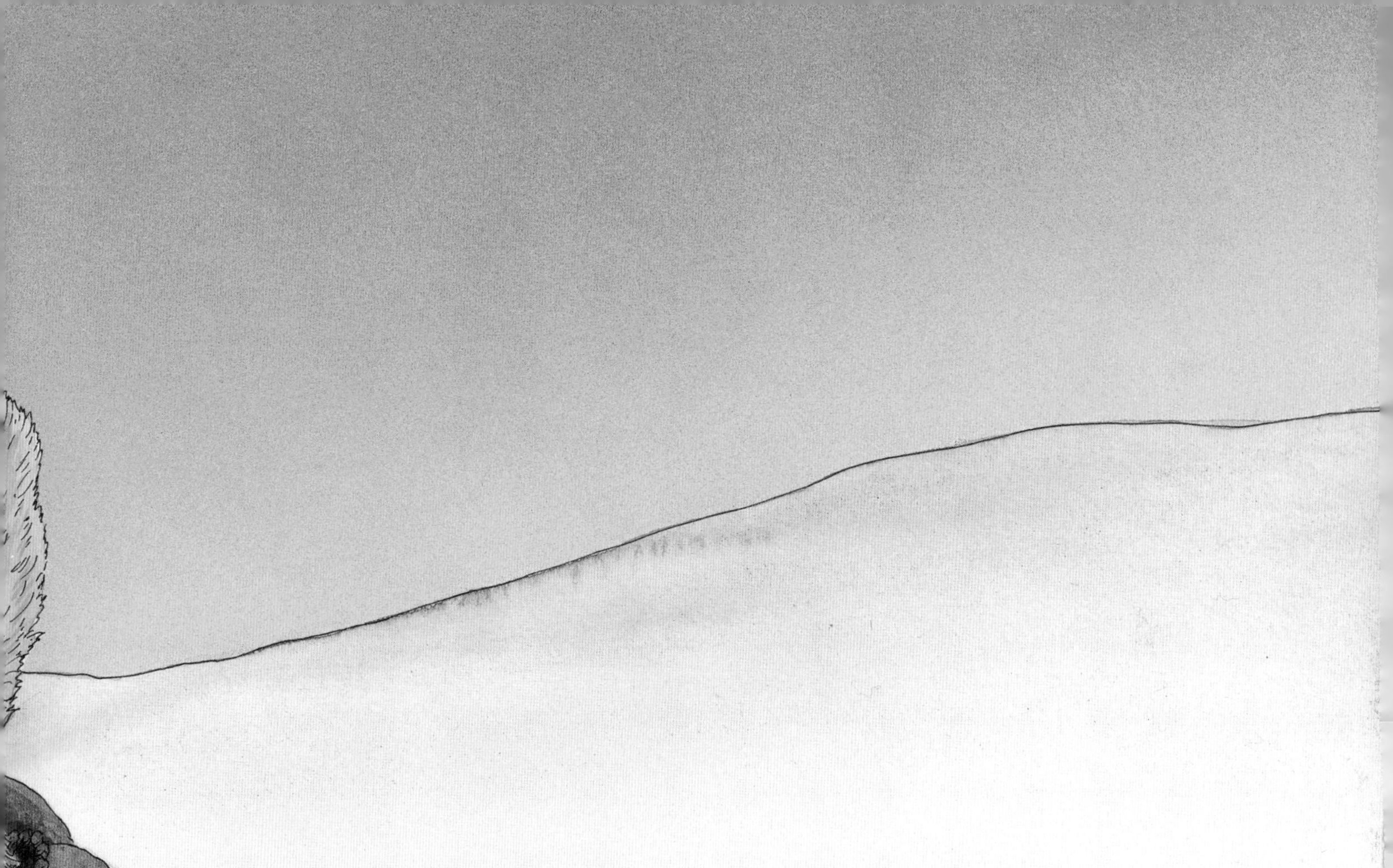

Liplap shivered. He peered hard at the snowbunny's face, then he dug down into the moist earth and found three shiny pebbles.

With the black stones he made two shiny eyes and a little black nose. Then with some pine needles he made the snowbunny's whiskers.

The snowbunny's eyes gleamed tiny lights from the last of the sun…then went dark. Something went dark inside of Liplap, too. He found a stick and carved a frown in the snowbunny's face. Then he hopped back into his house feeling very sad.

That night, Liplap's mother knelt
with him at the bedroom window.

"There's an old Rabbit's tale," she said,
"that your grandma used to tell. It's about
how, long ago, when the First Rabbits died,
they became stars in the sky. And to this day,
they come out at night and watch over us.
And they remind us that our loved ones
shine forever in our hearts. That's why
we wish upon a star."

"Do you think Grandma is a star?" asked Liplap.

"Well, look there," said his mother, pointing to the sky. "See that low star shining white — as white as Grandma's fur?"

"Do you think that's her?" asked Liplap eagerly.

"I think you could wish it were," answered his mother. Liplap closed his eyes and wished.

And when he opened his eyes, that white star seemed to wink and sparkle. It made him tingle.

"Now she's with us forever," he said, as he curled up in bed. Soon Liplap was dreaming.

The next morning, when Liplap hopped outside — *lip-lap, lip-lap* — he saw that the frown on the snowbunny's face had melted. In its place, Liplap stuck a carrot.

"Are you hungry, Snowbunny?" he asked. "*I* am."

Then Liplap ate *five* carrots — one for each point of a star.

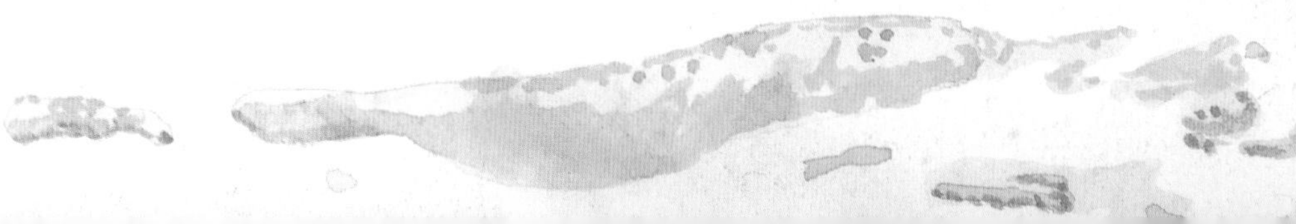